PLEASANT DREAMS
❧ Anna B. Francis ❧

Holt, Rinehart and Winston / *New York*

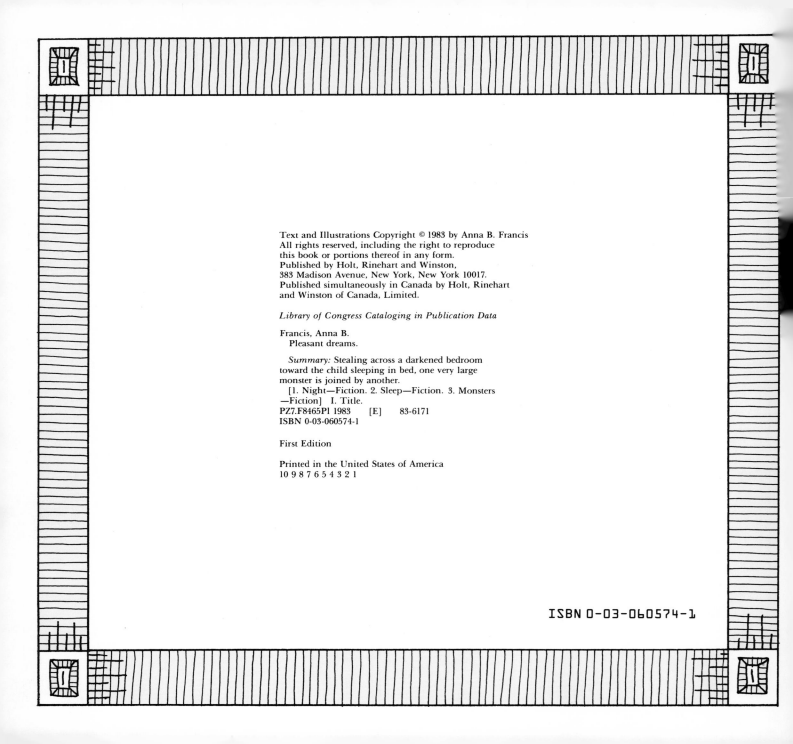

Published by Holt, Rinehart and Winston,
383 Madison Avenue, New York, New York 10017.
Published simultaneously in Canada by Holt, Rinehart
and Winston of Canada, Limited.

Library of Congress Cataloging in Publication Data

Francis, Anna B.
  Pleasant dreams.

  Summary: Stealing across a darkened bedroom
toward the child sleeping in bed, one very large
monster is joined by another.

  [1. Night—Fiction. 2. Sleep—Fiction. 3. Monsters
—Fiction] I. Title.
PZ7.F8465Pl 1983   [E]   83-6171
ISBN 0-03-060574-1

First Edition

Printed in the United States of America
10 9 8 7 6 5 4 3 2 1

ISBN 0-03-060574-1

To Sarah,
    for getting me started

To Stan and Ray,
    for keeping me going

and to Alex,
    for every day with love

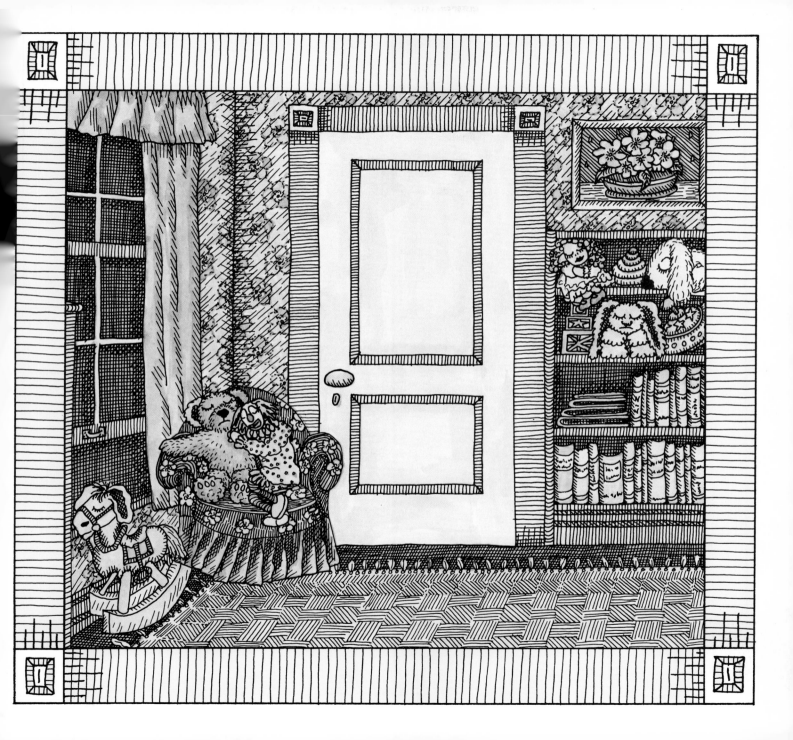

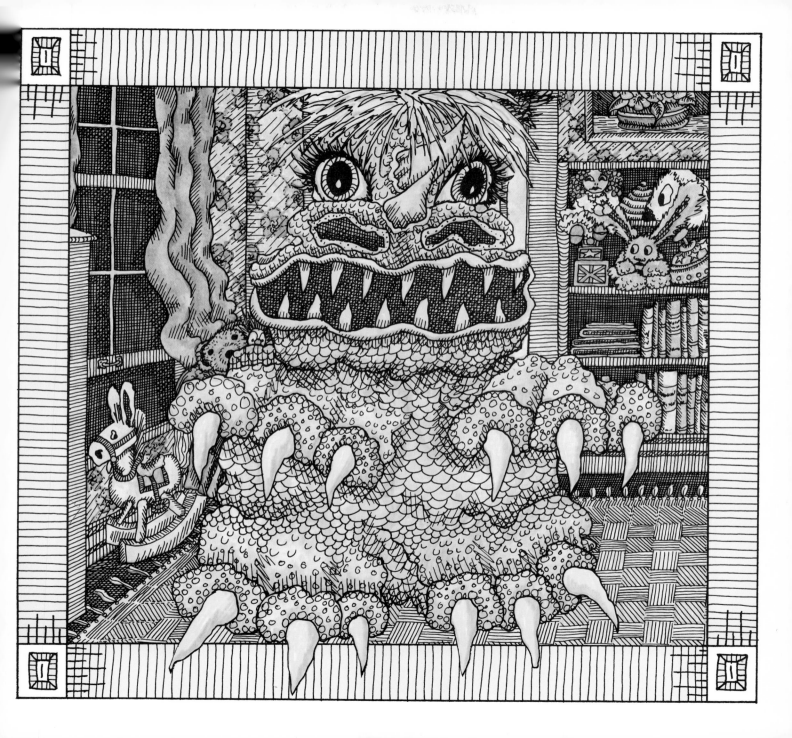

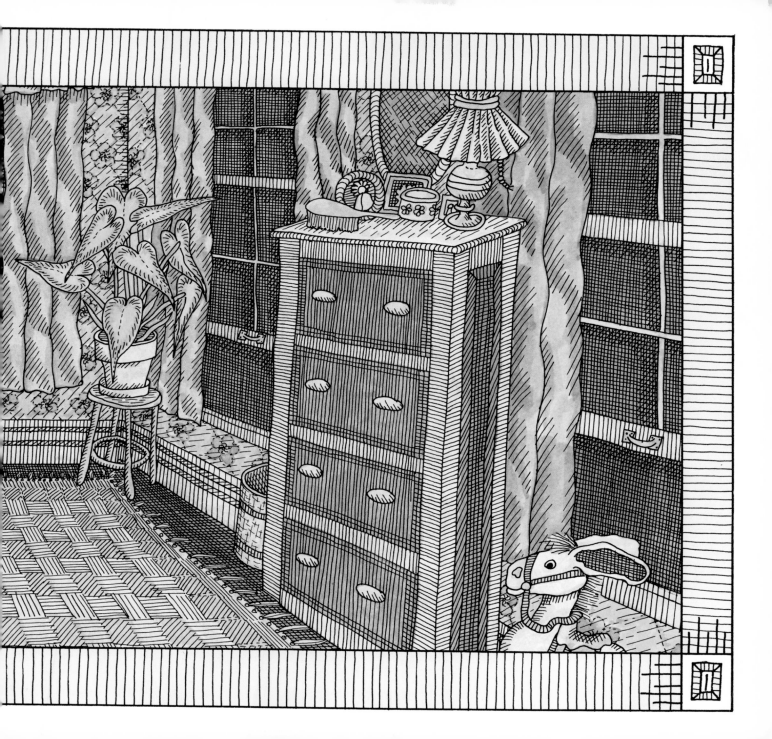

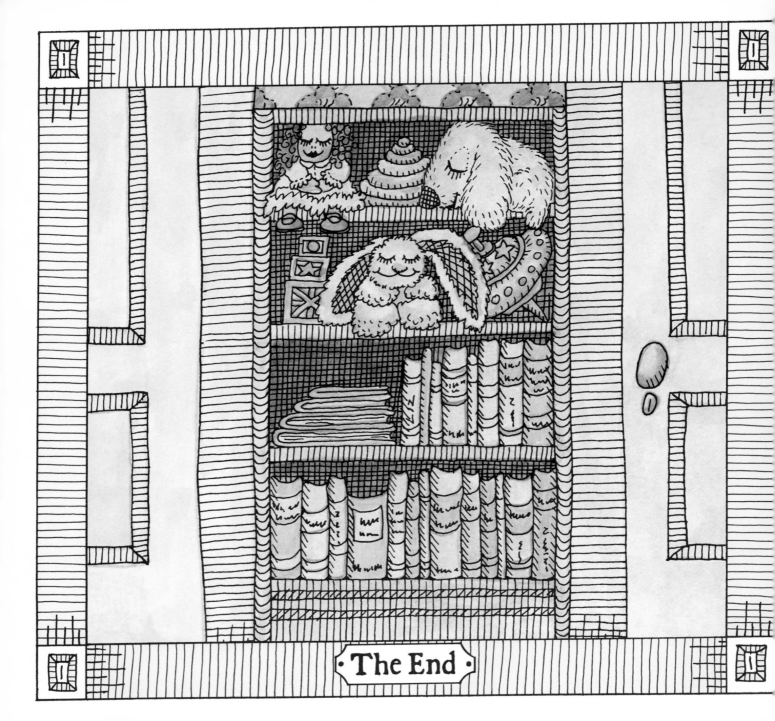

· The End ·